connecting medium

# acknowledgements

Acknowledgement is made to the anthologies in which the following poems first appeared: 'Connecting Medium' in *Word Up: Words from the Women's Cafe*, Centerprise, 1993; 'Meeting Mediums', in *Moving Beyond Boundaries*, Pluto Press, 1995; 'Milkdreams I & II' in *Burning Words, Flaming Images*, Saks Publications, 1996; 'Gambian Sting' and 'Medusa: Cuts both ways', in *Fire People: A Collection of Contemporary Black British Poets*, Payback Press, 1998; 'Five Strands of Hair' & 'Forget' in *Bittersweet: Contemporary Black British Women's Poetry*, The Women's Press, 1998; 'Faultlines' and 'Generations Dreaming I & II', in *Voice Memory Ashes: Lest We Forget*, Mango Publishing, 1999; 'Medusa? Medusa Black' in *Mythic Women/Real Women: Plays and Performances Pieces by Women*, Faber & Faber, 2000; 'c. 1950 Bubble n' Squeak' and 'c. 1967 Sweet Potato n'Callaloo', in *IC3: The Penguin Book of New Black Writing in Britain*, 2000

And to the following journals and magazines for 'Forget' and 'Medusa? Medusa Black!', in *Feed*, 1994; 'Faultlines' in *Writing Women*, 1995; 'Milkdreams' in *Scratch*, 1995; 'Connecting Medium', 'Medusa? Medusa Black!', in *Kunapipi*, 1995; 'Medusa: cuts both ways' in *Cutting Teeth*, 1996; 'Cross-roads: Junction 17 from 22' in *Cutting Teeth*, 1997; 'I'm in the Market for Hair', in *Calabash*, 1999; and 'Home', 'I'm in the Market for Hair' and 'Low Tide at Tendaba, in *Wasafiri*, 1999.

# connecting medium

## dorothea smartt

PEEPAL TREE

First published in Great Britain in 2001, reprinted 2011
Peepal Tree Press Ltd
17 King's Avenue
Leeds LS6 1QS

ISBN 9781900715508

Supported by
ARTS COUNCIL
ENGLAND

*Dedication*

To my maternal great-great-grandmother, and my parents Frederic and Ruby, for walking the path before me and lighting the way. To Sherlee Mitchell, for our shared journey and her loving creative support...

Thanks to

*Maferefun Orisa. Maferefun Egun.*
For the family-love of Jennifer Tyson, Ulanah Morris,
Sherlee Mitchell, Danny Abrahamovitch, and Myrna Bain.

*For your creative & spiritual sistahood:* Martina Attille,
Pamela Maragh, Elena Georgiou, Shay Youngblood, Donna
Weir-Soley, Marie-Alyce Devieux, & Keshia Abraham

*For their critical & editorial support:* Jacob Ross,
Bernardine Evaristo, Jeremy Poynting, with special grati-
tude to Kwame Dawes & the Afro-Style School.

*For creating possibilities:*
Apples and Snakes, Artsadmin, Arts Council of England,
Arvon Foundation, Audre Lorde Women's Poetry Center
(NYC), Black Arts Alliance, Black Women Talk publishers,
Brisons Veor, City Lit, Lois & Catherine (formerly of the
ICA) of the Live Art Development Agency, SAKS Media
Writers' Hotspots, Sauda, Spread the Word, Talawa Women
Writer's Project, and Ty Newydd.

*And to:* Adeola Agbebiyi, Adjoa Andoh, Audre Lorde,
Bryony Lavery, Carole Boyce-Davies, Delroy Williams, Joyti
Grech, Maud Sulter, Patience Agbabi, Jackie Kay, Joy
Russell, Kadija George, Lisbeth Goodman, Lorna Leslie,
Lois Weaver, Lydia Douglas, Madrina Teresa Ramirez,
Meredith Gadsby, Raman Mundair, Valerie Mason-John
and many others, for your belief, inspiration and support
along the way, with heartfelt thanks & nuff respect.

# contents

my name is many and in truth
without all parts I have no name at all...

> — Adjoa Andoh, "My True Name"
> in *Charting the Journey*, Grewal, S. et al,
> Sheba Feminist Publishers


She could work miracles, she would make a
garment from a square of cloth
in a span that defied time...

> — Lorna Goodison, "For My Mother"
> in *I Am Becoming My Mother*,
> New Beacon Books

# mother music

Listen, holy mother sounds combine, elevate
time in all its marvellous arithmetics to
pure moment that is. Now, how does the
drum sound suck me through skin down
to the bone? Stone bass chords rock me

to the bone-stone-bass. Chords rock me
on another journey to the one Mother, belly-
sounds daubing my ears. The broad Black
marker spurting booms and breaks to tattoo
the yolk of myself. Opening, resonating, vibrating.

The yolk of myself opening, resonating. Vibrating
story after story, after birth after life after death.
Music, a tick-tock back-drop tune
to the soul. Key into Spirit. Tempo emotion.
Music, the human obsession to sing to dance.

Music, the human obsession. To sing to dance
makes me want to holler sometimes, throw up
both hands to God. She is reworking her miracle
of creation everyday. Listen, holy mother
sounds combinating, elevating life

## generations dreaming I.

Journeywoman. Journeyman.
You were a generation dreaming;
journeywoman, journeyman,
stepping off the plane
to an unknown future
from a certain past that
became more and more like
the promise that escaped you.
You were a generation
dreaming to change the pattern,
undo the seams, re-style
the suits you wore
as you stepped off the boat,
Windrush-style.

Frederic: this not so young man
had struggled as a juvenile,
thirties-style, to unionize,
enfranchise. A troublesome man,
proud to be a darkblack
worker, survivor. You
split the seams
to suit your schemes.

Linda: journeywoman. Journeywoman,
you were a generation dreaming.
Coming from a certain past,
coming to an unknown future,
coming to bear us and
spare us from the masterpattern,
styled, cut, ready-to-wear suit
of canes, molasses

thick-set in the heat. Burning
good white sugar,
raising a glass of rum
in the sunset of the master
as you sailed away;
meeting this mancountry,
face-to-face with dreams.
Journeywoman, journeyman,
you were a generation,
dreaming a world, to change.

## generations dreaming II.

Your coming made me as I am,
not a Clarendon girl, or a
Bridgetown girl, but a
norf, sauf, west, east London
of a girl, even
a different kinda Essex girl,
the kinda Blackwoman
the world ain't seen yet.

With a stance, with words
that roll from me, telling
of West Indies trade,
England's sugar, and bitter cane;
trading culcha, trading food;
trading sounds and nuff expressions,

sweet bitter symphony,
here on her doorstep
in that tourist board land
of Beefeaters,
cheeky chirpy cockneys
bowler hats and butlers.

Turning swinging sixties, turning
skareggaedubtoastingsoulblack,
funkin for Jamaica, Barbados,
St Kitts, Nevis, St Lucia, St. Vincent, Montserrat,
Dominica, Antigua, Guyana, Grenada, Tobago,
Trinidad in streets of carnival
year after year,
as you cannot stop The Real Thing,
Aswad da'you know without us:

hundreds of thousand island voices
Mother      Father            Stories.

# faultlines

highbrown yellow red brownskin dark?
some nights I am awake and
wide-eyed as the full moon
though not as yellow
as my gran'mudder Estelle
a property-owning coloured
widda ten poun deposit
ope'nin a Barbados savings bank account
when white women were occupied
wid being ladies.
money to be made t'ru
panama canal years making silver men

highbrown yellow red brownskin dark?
my father in the white light of the moon
awoke to a sky teeming wid stars
that abandon him in Englan',
d'glare from
streets paved with gole
making it too light for stars
only the large but distant winter moon
remaining wide-eyed
and just as rich and yellow
set in a sparse sky,
the two inseparable like
mother and child
son to be exact

highbrown yellow red brownskin dark?
my father troublesome
with his shameful darkness
all wrong in a climate
where for the light almost white

the occupation of 'lady'
is almost within reach
and the pity of misfortune
with the judgement and expectation
of wrong-'e-all-wrong
an' baad-'e-too-baad
but whuyuh could x-spec'
from a literal black sheep
that when he rear up he own flock
the light yellow red
will have to pay –
they have it too easy.
he will shut a few doors
for the many that were slammed
in his way

sometimes I lie awake
in the shadow and light
of a moonlit night
wondering
at how the sins of the fathers
meet the unknowing child
and lie in wait
to slither between sisters
cocktailing with english days and ways
to break them up along colour lines
and continue in spite of itself
a silent contract down generations
to breed out the unseemly gloom
the get-you-nowhere stumbling darkness
and bestow the freedom of
lightskin  brownskin  highbrown
yellow red

## craving

I crave flavours I cannot find
without you.
I crave your voice flowing
stories no one else gave me,
sitting me down gently
to school and learn well.
I crave for fries
like my Daddie would make them,
pumpkin sweet in the morning,
or late at night
grating nutmeg into water and milk
chocolate boiling for a treat.
I crave your sweet bread
the smell of yeast and the breads
rising in d'pans
along with stories from Daddie
'bout the devil-dog
baby weddings
sunday school discord
'bout jumbies, shavers, and all
Bajan tings bumping
in a night without streetlamps,
only sweet clear moonlight
revealing crawling duppy crabs,
midnight shadows
chasing a speeding young boy
duppy on 'e tail
the soles of his feet
shining in the darkness
headlong up d'gap

# hagar's children

Count the navel strings tied.
Prayerbead. Mantrabead. Sweatbead

rolling down the body. Working
in the midday sun. Count

the bare-headed children
of Hajar. Protective

chants and spells all but gone.
Navel string        unattached.

# cut

When the moon was coming into blossom,
"Cut it then," she said. "It will grow back tall."
Spiked by the whip and the cutlass, chain-gang,

field-gang, pikney-gang, factory-gang gone.
But still it grows back. Straight back. In my face
are the shadows of evenings and dark nights

over there. Over here the same moon, full
of voiceless stories pressing to be told,
shrivel up, build up through generations

life severed, sliced by a moon beam, the first
and the last into a valley of death
they were driven. Back. "Cut it back," she said.
"They will grow tall and strong."

# cane

The roots in this woman
are countless navel strings

tied to apron strings, tied
bundles of cane stalks, tied

to the woman in front,
and the child tied behind.

Nascent roots. Boiling,
roots-working. This woman.

# middle passage

Middle passage clear now,
both ends open, to expel
debris from the hold.
Am I on the last leg
of your long journey started
when the moon was becoming,
so it would grow and grow
back? Take me back, take me back.
The roots of this woman
just one episode in history,
they say. Repeated like a mantra
                 like a dirge
                 like a praisesong
                 like a eulogy
                 like a curse,
one episode, told to shame me
and contain me:
Slavery – not a holocaust
or a genocide,
but tamed, maimed 'slave'
on reef rock and rolling sea
at Elmina.

# five strands of hair

## i. parting

I began clenched teeth,
tight steel combs and
mother's fingers —
slippery Dax heroines
pulled out the need.

Plaited and stocking-capped,
beside her head
the pungent edge of frying hair,
smoked brown-paper twists,
greased and combed.
Prevention is better than cure.

## ii. clueless

Her hair is straight
no twists or crosses

a wiped clean page
it doesn't read.

Curled out
no markers to ancestry —

that we have bad hair
that we have coolie in the family
that it tough and don't grow — no

see
her hair it's straight,
it doesn't read
easy.


## iii. twists and turns

Fact:   Your hair is an integral part of your skin.
Fact:   There is good hair, and there is bad hair.
Fact:   Hair and scalp diseases were common amongst enslaved Africans.
Fact:   A chemical used to straighten African hair is called 'lye'.
Fact:   Natural African hair must be processed to make it manageable.
Fact:   Black women spend a major part of their income fixing their hair.
Fact:   Straightening hair made the first U.S. Black millionairess.
Fact:   Black women need the hairdresser more often than white women.
Fact:   Different styles of plaiting and braiding marked rites of passage.
Fact:   Unkempt hair is a sign of madness.


## iv. a foreign head

She fetched
all through Sunday-best dinner.
Twisting and looking,
the question hovered round.
A well-raised Bajan girl,
she was too-too polite

until outside, bursting, she could
ask mummy-friend bigwoman dawter,
'You is a *rasta*?'


## v. revert

Still shouldering a Black Star Line,
he said no.
"Doan vex the children hair with foolishness".
His own balding masthead,
crowned with ancient mystery books,
the deep science
of pale-faded Egyptians –
the African headdress
bestowed away on me.

## denial

Remember
as a child I had a notion
that the wind
the sky
the trees
could be talked to
listened to, if you knew how
even ripples on the pond
at Battersea Park...

## black girl shuffle

no school no reason
to go outside
2-room 58 yelverton road.

banned from the lino
my white shoes shuffle
time-steps on a blackboard
doing my thing all summer
break on a small square space.

there was one bed
I lay in
made up for four
often sleeping one
or three but
I never slept alone.

our space kept us
tight – me and sis
we were one
of two-tapping feet
for this small girl someone
was always there –
a safe world.          home

on this syncopated space
bronze-medal  toes
tap my mind out of corners
skip, time-travel, glide
rhythms of worlds inside myself
sounding out time
stepping on a blackboard.

# forget

I don't remember a lot of things
quite deliberately shoving them away inside me
imploding later when I least expect
I don't remember
why should I
walk with it hold it know it
for all its unpleasantness feel it
choke me smoke me dope me
I don't remember is
my favourite reply when put on the spot
about how I got broken that time

I don't remember the sound
the jab of your words shattering me
as you chatted on dismissing a quiet plea
saying again don't be boring shuddering
as another piece hit the playground tarmac
spreading into a pool of once-me
trampled again and again
by my big sister's silences and refusals
to look me in the eye at least

I don't remember my wanting you
to do the enid blyton best friend thing and
rescue me from little girls that bullied me
or you bringing the taunting into our front-room
laughing at my swan neck, my cowardy-custard ways
I only remember the mirage of my hopeful fantasy
of ever-lasting super-glue love
like the infant fingers of that boy in my class
doing everything together
grown as one like twin plantains

that could never be parted with whole skin
that would not re-member itself
always being in half

I don't remember being unwanted
the day I ran out the school gate
away from the isolation of everybody else's eyes
witnessing another humiliation
to get away from – who
I don't remember
Mr Grant with his big six-foot army self
charging after me escorting me
an easy captive in biting April sleet
white as his big hand
leading up to the hair in his nose
a crowd of schoolkids telling me
I was really in trouble now
and the only eyes I wanted to see me were yours
away over at the other end of the playground
you wouldn't see me there

walking home I could never tell
feeling too shame in your this-isn't-happening-eyes
convenient forgetfulness stinging
from your mouth to the soothing front-door
our Yelverton Road home
where you were all the world I thought I needed

## carsons glucose factory, sw11

Mornin an evenin
it would cum on yuh
like a curse, seeping
all down York Road,

out belchin towers,
bringing up stink
from cane sweetness
burnin. Lorries passin,

leavin a trail writing
carsons glucose factory
in d'win — widda tail!
Yuh kyaan run from it!

It would move in yuh nose-
hole, squat an' let off
right here, durham buildings,
on d'lap of d'factory! Spewing
stench. Regular. Ev'ry day.

# home

when it began to get dark i realize this wasn't no joke
standing at clapham common. we still didn't have a place

moving round mum coat looking up at troubled voices
that had asked we two small girls break open our piggy

i wanted to find a goldmine in there, nuff brown coppers
to give us a home for the night. social services took us

to balham. more fretful hours in the warm waiting room.
would they rescue women and children first? leave us

fatherless for the night, waiting, falling asleep unsure of
the morning, who was in control, where to call home?

## cross-roads: junction 17 from 22

Early mornings, waking
on the verge of tears and
desperate for someone
to be with me, for her,
our flat missing a voice.
Thrust out of my boundaries,
tears first thing. I'm scared to
go out on my own. Stood
in front of my window,
looking at the largest
railway junction in the
world, with a train passing
every three minutes.
Wondering where to go.

## milkdreams

dripping milk baby's
mouth knows
only warmth comfort
and the sensation
of the breathing
heaving chest

your mother
spreads herself
before you
you cannot take her in
all at once
your head rolls off
and you are dreaming dreams
of her womb
still waters
still caressing you

# milkdreams ghost

*mum is that you?*
last night you came
back standing in the hall
your front
in her bedroom doorway
you stood naked
at the foot of the bed
spilling milk. dreaming
your daughter said
– stupid, like you didn't know –
*mum you haven't got any clothes on*

you gave her one look
to close her mouth
but her reverie still repeating
over and over
you frowned
until she got up
followed her mum's naked back down
stairs to the kitchen

now in your blue-white overalls
taking your girl outside to a yard
where there was none
and a big basin
water warm from a jamaican sun
looking at her
she was supposed to know
you wanted a daughter
now unsure of herself
reassured in sweetsmelling nutmeg
and handling milk

she thought she would drink
you pour it over her head
to spill down her face
pouring large
over your daughter's naked body
to dry in the sun

she woke up
to the sweetspice smell
of your just-baked cakes
still hanging around her
reassured and ready

## long night, portugal

My blood
traces either side
of the moon
twice a year
we collide
full blood-orange
hanging
onto the coast
of Lagos
in the early dawn sky

## moon

silver
in an indigo sea sky
your face rolled to one side
questioning the earth
and me
straining to see you
streetlevel
on a downtown
Manhattan skyscraper-line
I lose you repeatedly
behind
building after building
then the intermittent
renewals of your gaze
loving
always new
and I never grow tired
of seeing you

You laugh, you giggle. You fill me up so much! But still it ain't enough. And we both keep saying – *we shouldn't be gettin' on like this. Be sensible! You livin' with the woman you love. Me leavin' d' place in tree month.* But that don't change the feeling. Sparked by woman-chemistry, a look with those eyes is your hand between my thighs... So what – I'm leaving, you're staying here, and anyhow you're living with your lover. So what! The time is NOW so lets just go-with-the-flow and take it for what it is – Hot! We could be having fun with few strings attached. Heart first, dive in 'cause we have so little time. Let's just make the most of it. So what! SO WHAT can I stop a feeling this strong? 'Cause its inconvenient, not so tidy? 'Cause it wasn't meant to be like this. Although I'm looking for love – 'cause I keep finding it everywhere, there, and now, here with you! Wish with me – in the months to come such a friendship grows, y'know the kind where we could meet, anywhere, anytime and still be sensible for each other. In a passion that stands above and beyond the moment, an' we could make love, in a car, in a hallway, in a bathroom, in somebody else's upstairs room, outside inside. 'Cause through sighs an' moans, we just can't keep our hands to ourselves... *Jus' hole on! Y'know what y'saying? So what? What if...??* Well what if...??? Am I being foolish? Shall I live to regret this running-after-passion? I really don't think so...

## whirlwind

Sandstorms
let loose
by your whirlwind mouth
lash me
with words I don't recall.
It is safer
to keep inside
head down
safe
alone.

Sea of lights heading into J.F.K at night
scaled-up megamix
of everything I knew to be
industrial, urban
i started my period on the descent
hunter moon following me
reflecting in a winding river below
guiding me
thru' sets off t.v. cop shows
and a Black bourgeoisie
the town of Harlem
up Lennox to 132nd

## meeting mediums

a round faced sistah
all in white
opened the door

between two of them
swept away
feeling like a girl-child
trying to keep up

conversation flying
in and over my head
so many questions
I don't begin to ask

the unfamiliarity of my surroundings
silences me.

early
this morning
I remembered the glass fish
in my West-Indian home, typical
in shades of blue green and brown
when I was how old I don't recall
I took the fish
put pennies in its mouth
did this whole little ritual in 'african'
did this on my own in the front-room
maybe I was home
sick from school
maybe
I was home-sick.

## easy: banjul, the gambia

this country moves slowly
like my blood the first day
comes on little by little
the river before the moon peaks
pours herself out
heavy with life
cleansing unplugged
i flow sienna
drift
*kamari*
like the moon
this country paces herself
each day
moves in her own good time
like me
there's no rush of blood
just slow pulsing
easy

## gambian sting

A Gambian sting left her in Kwinella.
No money, no passport, nothing.
These brothers know what to say, run it like
a pre-recorded tape: play-pause-rewind.

No money, no passport, nothing!
These guys had promised overstanding,
said, "Yes, Rasta sistah!" smiling at her
dreads. Said, "Yes, you are home, in Africa."

These 'brothers' know what to say, run it like
a life line between me and the longing
they read in my eyes, the restless ghosts
of unspeakable times jostling for redemption.

A Gambian sting. Left her in Kwinella
at the base of a silk cotton tree.
Tears washing the red ochre, dusting her feet,
spirits thronging to give salvation to the restless.

A Gambian sting left her in Kwinella.
No money, no passport, nothing!
These brothers know what to say, run it like
a pre-recorded tape: Play. Pause. Rewind
the lash, the sting marking us both.

# by river gambia

I

wind brushing my face
creases the river lifts vultures
off tree branches

II

earth tipped over
the river's waters sail out
make sea waves tidal

III

wind snatching my words
river gambia swallows them
ink runs up river

# low tide at tendaba

riverside rocks crawling
with baby-small crabs
their larger white spur
beckoning the sun
'over here'
claws tug my eyes

sideways
they amble their way
across the glassy mud
freckled by pebbles
far mangrove trees stranded
on their roots
calling a curved fringe of water
spread out in
wavy froths
like a shoal of white fish
playing

sack-billed pelicans glide
air-streaming
low and assured bodies
over the muddied river-sea

the sun and the wind
the feel of drum and brush song
always calls the rains

in this dry season
these waters are out of range
the breeze flutters-cool my skin

sun snares my eyes
beating light into my high noon
before the hour is out
copper earth waves
run their way back to shore
bringing me
riverside

## mr. watchman

mr. watchman knows the times. eyewitness.
strange behind glasses and endless time-pieces.
set up near the market cross, he eyes them,
one time. any day was a bustling trade, now
it's only saturdays that bring the people out
full-of-life, lighting electric avenue. crowds
hustle through the nineties, a smooth sight.
mr. watchman: seer of the seasons, changes.
stop. watch he's marking time
as the market never lean or clean
is going
going
going
on

# c.1950 - bubble n' squeak

In post-war days
market barrows bubble
and squeak under 'English'
potatoes and cabbage. Heads
in flat-caps, with sack aprons,
old men trundle. Handling
sure and swift full baskets
of turnips and swedes
fresh from the counties,
4d a pound. Savoy cabbage
complexions with
cauliflower ears
and parsnip noses transport loads
even in rain and smog,
their market boots
carrying their feet,
over charcoal silver cobbles.

## c.1967 – sweet potato n' callaloo

After Parkes Drugstores came
Timothy Whites and now
by Boots, on the corner
of Electric Avenue,
they're selling soul food.

Strange at first, but
slowly came a liking for
Jamaica's patties.
Opened the way to foreign roots
formed into 'Back Home Foods'
eddoes and ackees
sweet potatoes and callaloo.

Faces reach from scarves,
head-tied against the cold.
In days ahead, bustling
for cow-feet and pig-tail,
the women offer open bags
for warmer foods to tumble into.

## shopping on a vision quest

In revelation, arcades open
making a welcome
with familiar arms.
For the tall Bajan man,
the Jamaican woman
in the universal space
a ritual meeting
at the foot of altars
of green coconuts, green
mangoes, green bananas
peeling back layers
of forgetfulness,
enabling a clearer vision.

Shopping: on a vision quest.

## haiku to electric avenue

In the market place

thought creates magic
tattooed on a bare breast bone
the eye of Horus.

in the market place

a first light marvel singing
an electric avenue
makes this body shine.

## the linen baba

To set up house – the linen baba would sort you out.
He'd understand; he'd come, you see,
from Pakistan in sixty-two.
Selling on deposit blankets for the cold,
door-to-door, until a countryman said:
there's Market Row instead.

Aurora towels, bright parchment linen,
clouds of quilts and misty mosquito nets
high up on the ceiling. A home store
for a generation of sojourners who came
expectant, filled with respect.

Baba, aging now, held up by crisp Sundays
(best tablecloths and arm-rests)
retired from being in the market everyday,
now sees friends' and old customers' children
come to shop, emerging bright from
his stalls' linens and quilts.

# the holy shop

"This one small stall could save a town",
accessorizing hallelujahs in service to the Lord.
For tabernacle, lodge or chapel, a glorious crown

of candles and crucifixes. In Reliance, on boards,
saints and saviours line the walls. Reaching out
to noisy strangers, his clasped hands a ford

across arcade sounds raised to a shout,
chorus of confusion round this meeting-stall of rest.
A highway to heaven – they come from all about

to the Russian Ottone. First fancy goods, then a test –
chalk busts of saints beginning the shop's conversion,
joined in Christ, in religious, and spiritual zest.

Long-standing customers inspirit in their assertion:
'This holy shop's protected' in any Metropolitan uprising
of 'Sus' on the streets to put down subversion.

Here's a place of peaceful communion, for unburdening
under the ears of Yemoja, as the Virgin. Here's retail
therapy (in Christ we trust) to move a soul to healing.

## dance with me

Live souls of music-makers
work me into dance styles.
From our dispersion they come.
Out of me, above, below,
sounds zest through me.
Improvising, I move. My body knows the score.
Rhythms ooze through, pouring.
I am
possessed. I see
with my body, separating
from wherever
I am.
I move
into the music.
The music moves
into me – we come together,
I want it inside me, deep
deep. It's there! Just there! Don't stop,
don't stop, yes, yes, yes! Ummm....
Then
we ride again,
bassline calling me out,
calling
praises from my body.

# I'm in the market for hair

I, head down and under wraps,
make for the hair express convenience,
a place to market changes to maps

routing their way to Africa. With reverence
for style, innovation, re-creation, I am heir
to products for my fleece's convalescence.

She says, "We're all women and we all share
this deep-rooted concern to secure and shape
'Beautiful Beginnings' for our children's hair."

As for myself, I'll be a riot of colour. Drape
'Sleek Wigs' on my head, a daring new version
where hotcombs failed to tread. Take

'Pride of USA' and 'L.A. Trend' for my conversion
to a new cartography. Weaved against reversion.

## ten paces

I fear
if I could turn men to stone
I'd walk round
beside
in front
but never
behind them.

# medusa? medusa black!

Medusa was a Blackwoman,
afrikan, dread
cut she eye at a sista mirror
turn she same self t'stone.
She looks really kill?
Ask she nuh! Medusa would know.
She terrible eyes leave me stone coal.
Medusa lost
looking for love
kept behind icy eyes
fixed inside the barricade
for anybody who come too close,
runnin' from she own
in case the worse thing happen
an' she see she self like them see she.
The blood haunted:
if you black, get back
if you brown stick around...
Is that okay? Being black your way,
whitewashed an' dyed-back black,
am I easier to hold in an acceptable role?
...And if you white comelong y'alright...
Make it go away, the nappiheaded nastiness
too tuff too unruly too ugly too black
...Get back...
Scrub it bleach it operate on it powder it
straighten it fry it dye it perm it
turn it back on itself
make it go away make it go away.
Scrub it, step smiling into baths of acid
and bleach it red raw
peel skin of life-sustaining melanin.
Operate on it

blackskin – lying, useless – discard it powder it.
Head? Fuck it, wild-haired woman,
straighten it fry it, desperately burn scalps.
Banish the snake-woman
the wild-woman
the all-seeing-eye woman.
Dye it,
remembrances of Africa fast-fadin'
in the blond highlights,
turn us back on ourselves
slowly making daily applications
with our own hand.
My hair as it comes
is just not good enough.
The blood haunted:
if you black get back
if you brown stick around
and if you white comelong y'alright…
Say: make it go away make it go away
da nappiheaded nastiness!
Is too tuff too unruly too ugly too black
too tuff too unruly too ugly too black.
Get back
Medusa! Black! [*Steups!*] Get back.

## medusa: cuts both ways

Dread!
An Afrikanwoman
full of sheself
wid dem dutti-eye looks
sapphire eyes
Yes nuh! believe it!
she could turn a man t'stone
some whiteman
nightmare riding
he mind across the centuries
in turn turning we mad

Medusa
dread anger
welling up in her stare
natural roots Blackwoman
loving Blackwomen
serious

He'd be frighten fuh dat
mark wid d'living blood
that bleeds and never dies
turns blood our sweet honey
from a rock
yes, that is sum'ting
would frighten any man

And still it goes on and on and on
around us inside us
their voices
whistling against
our thunder
across an eternal sky

Medusa is Nanny
Medusa is Assata Shakur
Medusa is Cherry Groce
is Eleanor Bumpers                    is Audre Lorde
is Queen Nzinga        Sarraounia
QueenMother            is godmother
                       our mother
Medusa is our mother's mothers
                       myself all coiled into one
Medusa is spirit
Medusa in you is you in me
                       is me in you
Medusa is my shield
impregnable
my aegis —
no mythical aegeanpeople shield
this is my armour
with Shango double-headed axe
Yemoja-Ocuti
my battle dress armour
of serious dread

# dream bed

Medusa sleeps in old furniture
head deep in her pelvis
modelling clay.
Her hair would grow
righthanded. Snakes hung, glorious.
Medusa's visions
make pillows
that prop her up.
Her head, hair,
her womb folds
up a hidden cavern.
Reach in, under her back door,
turn past pages.
Reflect, research the truth
down under covers.
Tell her stories –
cool paintbrushes
to frame, colour, touch.
And sometimes silk
flecks of orange come
to where in winter
she could be black, serpentine.

## medusa dream

Perseus comes. Full of intent
to carve out a name for himself in blood,
sent on a mission to claim her head.
Swindles her kind, never plays straight,
comes in confusion, proclaiming he knows it all,
tricks his way to the mouth of Medusa's cave and
cannot look in her face.
He takes out a mirror to see what he hopes for
and butchering her image captures her head,
spectacle to dishonour
prophet of the grotesque.
He sees what he wants, he wants her
shimmering in the dark
a head full dread full
confusion


All through that night, changing winds had blown. Medusa could not
see the moon, full as it was. Horseman behind her. She had not seen
him. He watched. He rode silent, up behind her. She had lain restless,
restless between trees.

Medusa dreamt:

*She is with her mother on the bed. Her mother is under
the bedclothes. She sits on top of them, desperate. Her
mother is not moving and she desperately needs to shit.
But before she lifts off the bed, it slides, landing solid. She
is so ashamed, but relieved – that it dropped out hard and
dry enough to remove without trace, she hopes. She
searches around for something to lift it with. It's repulsive
and she holds her breath, swallows and braces herself to
pick it up with her bare fingers. She runs with it to the*

toilet, banging open the door, straight onto her father's knees. He's sitting, doing what she had done – but in the right place for it. She's embarrassed, he's ashamed. He pushes the door, she knows she should not be seeing him like this, but has this thing in her hand, her shit in her fingers! She has to be rid of it. So she leans over him and drops it into the bowl. They are both crying, ashamed, belittled, without dignity... Then he gestures to his daughter to help him. He holds his penis, and pulling, peeling the foreskin, shows her how sore it is. The soft flesh has split, the great flaming sore bristles – red and raw. He's pleading. She cries again. For his shame, not hers.

And waking, it was then she sensed something. Something very wrong.

Medusa could feel her hair, held up tight-fisted.
She looked around, but could see nothing, no one.
Looking to the ground she saw
her body without a head, trembled and shook.
It was then she screamed, and the blood pumped out of her.

# medusaspeak

Trying to save the life
that is one's own,
white foaming at her
mouth, Medusa screams for
you to hear her.

Her granite lips crash
across teeth, sharper
cries roar foaming,
cross her meaning
lost on the wind.

You turn
run afraid.
You refuse to be alone
with her
Your terror leaves
Medusa standing, molten
tears across her rockface.
How can she speak to you
gently of hard things?

Every monster has her place.
A simple truth
she comes to tell,
this shadow from
the beacon,
the source, the god-send, the dark,
the truth.
Who's 'she'?
Honey,
sweet honey,
you are.

Here she is
standing ready
to rip        to claw      to beat
you to your monster self.
Narrow the focus
block the light.
In your own tall shadow
crouch        quiver        whimper.
Let your hair grow long. Rage
down to skin and bone. Rage
red-hot-blue-cold
tearing you. Solitary in the dark.

## let her monsters write

Medusa squeezes herself into
irregular-sized compartments,
wooden and fortress-like,
cosy and difficult and too small
to tuck in her frilly outstretched
body. Surrounding her is
an older I, her centre cave.
Under hair
let her monsters write
from all sides – ceiling walls floor.
Make a deep welcome
for this singsong body
lacy in the night.

## way to go

generations dreaming
words change
but the song of death is
life
our parents live
two lives to death
circling souls
along the road
we have come a long way
and still have a way to go
souls like faces come back
from you to me
to you the backbeat
our parents' voices
well-travelled imaginations
press us with manifestations
but we are mistrustful
hard-ears children
existing on our own
when ascendant generations
clamour to us
to speak with our light

listen!
guardian voices range around us,
slow pupils to the spirit

# let me land...

Rattling, far out, memories recurring,
patterns snake, rippling through the diaspora,
living down a cruel telling
seized by remembered words-of-mouths.

Imagine yourself from outside, uniquely terrible,
softly shimmering, swelling under a seascape,
the Caribbean waters' first light,
dark turquoise broken only by the breeze.

Waves spring from the sea-green
becoming high-riding watershaking locks
Herself and Medusa re-membered,
leaping and falling in ordered confusion,
soft and violent, slow and sudden,
and always the roaring spread of the wide overriding main.

Imagine yourself, from outside,
uniquely terrible, darkly shimmering locks
fallen to clouded land
slapped by cold on wet, the uniform grey skies.
Their eyes flame lava patterns on skins.
They alight, uncoiled from the diaspora.

Conjuring stones,
incantations rumble; rocks groan, rocks quake,
seized by remembering,
stones swell humming their birth.
Hear their voices; mining seams
beyond the rockface,
lithic jewel eyes, reincarnating powers.

Herself, in stone, Medusa, in stone.
Repelling, mud-slides over their heartfossil canyons.
Each having her metamorphic store,
shadow crevices raucous with crystal coal,
and the chance to burn.

Earth.

No words yet, just sounds; wind
sea spray, distant thunder announce them.
Inside the mist their tide laps in
and these two, Herself & Medusa,
are coming ashore

## about the author

Dorothea Smartt, born and raised in London, is of Barbadian heritage. Her work as a poet and live artist receives critical attention in both Britain and the U.S.A. She is acknowledged as tackling multilayered cultural myths and the real life experiences of Black women with searing honesty. She was Brixton Market's first Poet-in-Residence, and a former Attached Live Artist at London's Institute of Contemporary Arts, and a Guest writer at Florida International University and Oberlin College, U.S.A.

Dorothea Smartt is a working poet, with a wealth of experience as a creative writing facilitator and mentor. She is also poetry editor of SABLE Litmag, and co-Director of Inscribe, a creative & professional development project for Black & Asian writers. Described as "accessible & dynamic", her work has been selected to promote the best of contemporary writing in Europe today. Dubbed 'Brit-born Bajan international' (Kamau Braithwaite), her first poetry collection *connecting medium* (2001, Peepal Tree Press), is highly praised as the work of "...A master artist who sculpts both Standard and Caribbean English into a variety of poetic forms... capable of boldly crossing cultural boundaries" (*Caribbean Writer*), it also features a Forward Poetry Prize 'highly commended poem', and includes poems from her outstanding performance works "Medusa" and "From You To Me To You" [An ICA Live Art commission]. She's read and performed as a live artist, both nationally and internationally, and enjoys going into schools. Her next installation [video/ poetry text] will feature at the Museum in Docklands, London as part of the international exhibition "Landfall" in February 2009.

# Other views

...witty, caught up, fresh and connected. A new generation...

dr. mary hanna, university of the west indies (mona)

Some of the most exciting poetry being written in England today... highly intuitive yet precise...one of the evening's highlights.

lauri ramey, konch

Straight down the line, Dorothea Smartt shoots it past you...the pulse of her work rises and falls...images make noise, silences are transformed.

konrad keno foster, caribbean times

One of the most daring and exciting figures to emerge from London's poetry scene ... constantly experiment(ing) with both the form and content of her work, tackling the themes of identity, alienation and self-fulfilment with refreshing boldness.

apples and snakes

A powerful black woman making herself heard... Smartt offers images... which are realistic and mythical, deadly serious and wryly ironic.

lisbeth goodman, modern drama

"She writes within a tradition of artists working and re-working diasporic connections ... precisely so that, continuously enriched and informed by an active past, Black people can face the world as our own subjects."

maxine miller, lambeth librarian